For my little chick Lucas, I looked forward impatiently to your birth and love you very much. — Loufane

First published in Belgium and Holland by Clavis Uitgeverij, Hasselt – Amsterdam, 2013
Copyright © 2013, Clavis Uitgeverij

English translation from the Dutch by Clavis Publishing Inc. New York
Copyright © 2016 for the English language edition: Clavis Publishing Inc. New York

Visit us on the web at www.clavisbooks.com

Vincent the Impatient Chick written by Thierry Robberecht and illustrated by Loufane
Original title: *Vincent het ongeduldige kuikentje*
Translated from the Dutch by Clavis Publishing

ISBN 978-1-60537-196-2

This book was printed in February 2016 at Publikum d.o.o., Slavka Rodica 6, Belgrade, Serbia

First Edition
10 9 8 7 6 5 4 3 2 1

Thierry Robberecht & Loufane

Vincent

the Impatient
Chick

Clavis

NEW YORK

When **Vincent** opens his eyes in his egg, it's dark as night. He hears his mother's soft voice saying: "Just **a bit more patience**, little one, you have **all the time** in the world to be born. Stay in the warm egg a little longer. Wait."

But **Vincent** can't be calm;
he's a **restless chick**.
The last thing he wants is to sit in the
dark. He wants to see his mommy,
and he can't wait. That's why he starts
to tap the eggshell with his beak.
He makes small holes that let in
the light. "Oh…" he whispers,
"a sky filled with stars!"

"**Wait, my darling**,"
Mommy says, worried.
"You're still too **small**.
You don't have enough strength
yet to break your own egg...."
But **Vincent** wants to know
what is happening in the world.
He wants to see the light.
And his mommy, of course.

That's why he taps his beak, harder and harder, until the egg finally breaks.
And that is how *Vincent* the **restless** chick is born.
He is the first one. None of the other eggs even have a crack yet.
"Hi Mommy," *Vincent* says. "I'm here!"
"Hello, my sweet *impatient* boy," says his mother, and she smiles.

Vincent is bored. What's keeping his brothers and sisters?
Every so often he pushes their eggs and calls:
"**Come on**, come out already and play with me!"
"Calm down, *Vincent*, they have to gather their strength
in their eggs before they can be born," Mommy explains.
Two days later all the brothers and sisters have left their eggs.
"**None too soon**," *Vincent* says.

Soon **impatient _Vincent_** wants to eat big juicy worms.
"Vincent, my sweet boy, you're still **too small** to do that!
Eat delicious grain, like your brothers and sisters."
"No," Vincent the foodie answers, "I want big worms,
because my older brothers and sisters eat them."

Without thinking **Vincent** tries to pull a big worm
out of the earth. But the worm pulls harder
and disappears back under the ground.
Vincent didn't even get a tiny bite!

Vincent is too **impatient** to be sleeping in Mommy's warm nest. He thinks he is **big enough** to sleep with the other chickens on the perch. "Stay here, my darling," Mommy warns, "you'll get a cold on that perch!"

But *Vincent* is a stubborn chick. He jumps and jumps, but he can't reach the perch. His wings are **too small** and his legs are **too short**. **He can't jump high enough**. Grumbling, he returns to Mommy's nest.

Vincent wants to go to school with his big brothers and sisters. "You stay here," Mommy says. "You're still **too small** to go to school. Maybe in a year or two."
"A year or two?! That's **way too long**!"
Vincent objects. "I want to go to school now!"

When Mommy isn't looking, brave *Vincent* sneaks out.
He runs after his big brothers and sisters because he wants to go to school.
But he can't keep up. His little legs are **too short** and the older chicks run
too fast. After a while *Vincent* gets lost. He is all alone in the big woods.
Somewhere a branch creaks....

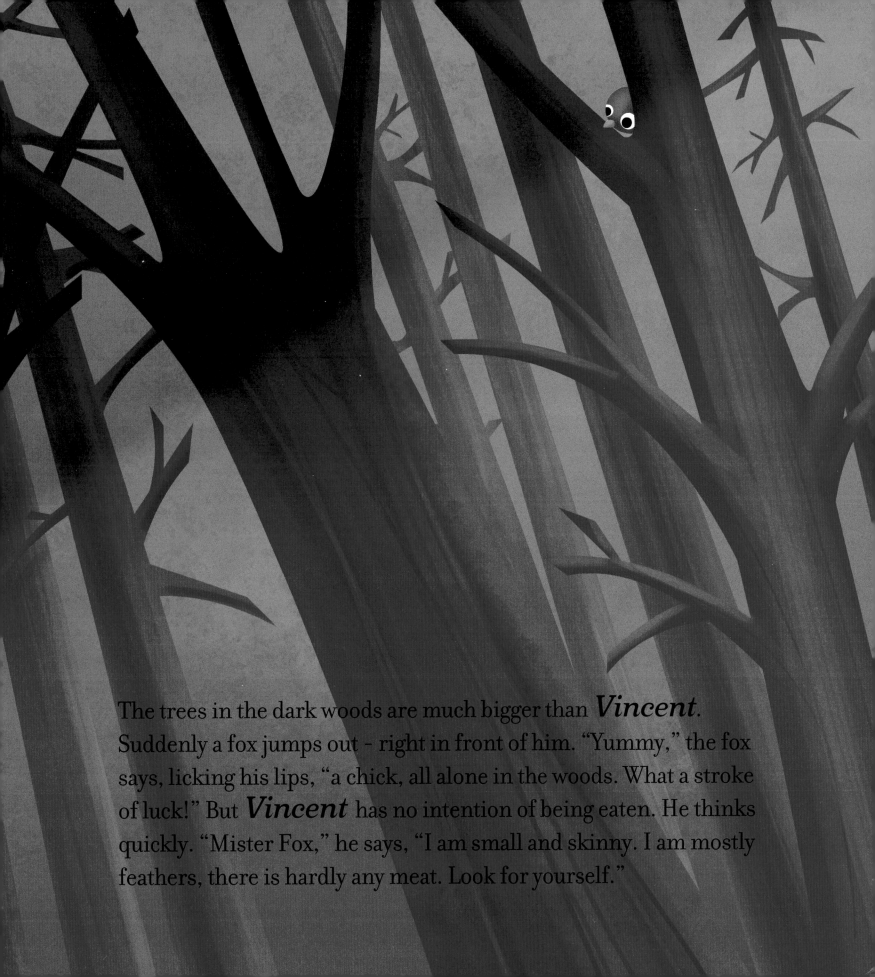

The trees in the dark woods are much bigger than *Vincent*.
Suddenly a fox jumps out - right in front of him. "Yummy," the fox
says, licking his lips, "a chick, all alone in the woods. What a stroke
of luck!" But *Vincent* has no intention of being eaten. He thinks
quickly. "Mister Fox," he says, "I am small and skinny. I am mostly
feathers, there is hardly any meat. Look for yourself."

The fox is confused. He's not sure he's very hungry anymore. Will a small chick like that taste good? While the fox is thinking, *Vincent* sneaks away. He runs through the bushes as fast as he can. After a while he finds the way back home. Luckily. Phew, that was close. From now on he will listen to Mommy.

Now **Vincent** is a beautiful young rooster. He eats big worms, roosts with the chickens and walks to school through the woods. Every morning he **waits impatiently** for the sun to come up. He can't crow until it does. "Come on, sun, a bit faster, please!" he calls out. And the sun replies with a sigh, "**Vincent**, dude, you're the most **impatient** rooster I have ever met!"